Gogo and the Upside Down Umbrella

Kathy Hill

AuthorHouse™ UK
1663 Liberty Drive
Bloomington, IN 47403 USA
www.authorhouse.co.uk
Phone: 0800.197.4150

Published by AuthorHouse: 08/01/2017

ISBN: 978-1-5246-8317-7 (sc)
ISBN: 978-1-5246-8316-0 (e)

Print information available on the last page.

Any people depicted in stock imagery provided by Thinkstock are models,
and such images are being used for illustrative purposes only.
Certain stock imagery © Thinkstock.

This book is printed on acid-free paper.

Because of the dynamic nature of the Internet, any web addresses or links contained in this book may have changed
since publication and may no longer be valid. The views expressed in this work are solely those of the author and do not
necessarily reflect the views of the publisher, and the publisher hereby disclaims any responsibility for them.

authorHOUSE®

For Q. W.
and for E.Y., who, she
assures me,
is entering her second childhood.

This is a story about Q and Gogo.
Gogo is Q's Granny, Q calls her Gogo.
Gogo is the Zulu word for Granny.
You have to say it "Gor Gor," like "or or",
with a G.

"Let's go to the park", said Gogo.
"Cheese!" said Q.
Q always says cheese when he is happy.
"Hmm" said Q's Daddy, "it looks like rain".
"I'll go in my rain bubble" said Q.
"I will wear my boots and take my umbrella"
said Gogo.

"Ok" said Daddy, "I have to prepare for my gig tonight. Be back before tea, Mummy will be home early."

So Gogo and Q set out for the Park.

On the way to the park a big dark cloud suddenly appeared overhead and the wind started to blow really hard.

Big drops of rain started to fall on Gogo's umbrella and on Q's rain bubble.

"Eesh!" shrieked Gogo.

"Eek!" squealed Q, "let's go home Gogo!"

But the wind was blowing so hard Gogo couldn't hear Q in his rain bubble.

Suddenly a BIG gust of wind turned Gogo's umbrella upside down and lifted Gogo and Q off the ground and up into the air.

Up up up they flew, high into the dark cloud.
"Hold on Gogo!" shouted Q.
"Holi Canoli!" shouted Gogo.
But Gogo and Q couldn't hear each other above the roar of the wind.

Just when Gogo thought she couldn't hold on any longer the wind died down and the sun came out and a big blue round house appeared in the sky.

There were flowers in blue bottles and little birds splashing in little puddles of water.
"Look at that Gogo!" cried Q.
"I wonder who lives here?" said Gogo.

Just then the door opened and a little round blue man came out. He had a very big moustache and round blue spectacles.

"Hello Gogo, hello Q" he said.

"Hello" said Q,
"Hello" said Gogo, "you sound as if you are talking under water."
"That's because I am made of water" said the blue man. "I am Mr Raindrop. Come inside and have tea you must be cold and wet."
"I am rather" said Gogo.
"I am alright in my rain bubble" said Q.
"Well you won't need it anymore" said Mr Raindrop, "You can fold it up and store it in your buggy".
So Gogo and Q went into the blue house.

Sitting at the table was a little round blue lady. She had a very big apron and round blue spectacles.

"I am Mrs Raindrop she said, welcome to our home, what would you like for tea?"

"Cheese" said Q, "and apple juice."

Then he remembered and said "Please."

"Do you have Redbush tea?" asked Gogo.

"We have everything you want here" said Mrs Raindrop.

"I would like a piece of milktart please" said Gogo.

"This is the best cheese!", said Q.

"This is the best milktart!" said Gogo, "but why do you live up here?"

"We are the Rain People" said Mr. Raindrop. "We know when the land needs rain and we call the wind and the dark clouds and we send our Rain drop family to water the flowers and trees and fill the dams and rivers so people and animals don't get thirsty".

"You must miss your Raindrop family very much" said Gogo.

"We do" said Mrs Raindrop, "but when the plants and animals and people have enough water, we call the Sun and she works her magic to bring all our family of Raindrops back home."

"Until they have to water the flowers again" said Q.
"You are very clever young man" said Mr Raindrop.

"That's a lovely story Gogo," said Q.
"Yes" said Gogo, "but we need to get back now, Mummy is going to be home soon."
"Do we have to go back through the dark cloud?" asked Q.
"Ho ho oh no" said Mr Raindrop, "I have an idea!"
He opened the door and there was a shiny rainbow reaching all the way to the ground.

"Goodbye Mr and Mrs Raindrop" said Gogo, "Thank you for the tea." said Q, "I had the best cheese."
And with that Q and his buggy and Gogo and her upside down umbrella slid all the way down the rainbow and into Q's backyard.
"Holi Canoli!" shouted Gogo.
"Cheese!" shouted Q.

"I am glad you didn't get caught in the rain" said Daddy, "you must be hungry."
"I had the best cheese" said Q.
"I had the best milktart" said Gogo.

"Hello!" called Mummy, "I'm home."
"Cheese? Milktart?" asked Daddy, "where did you have tea?"
But Q and Gogo had already run upstairs.

The End

49741388R00015

Made in the USA
Middletown, DE
21 October 2017